To Leo

from

Kathy Caple

January 2000

Starring HiLLARY

Kathy Caple

CAROLRHODA BOOKS, INC./MINNEAPOLIS

Carolrhoda Books, Inc. c/o The Lerner Publishing Group
241 First Avenue North, Minneapolis, MN 55401 U.S.A.

Website address: www.lernerbooks.com

Library of Congress Cataloging-in-Publication Data

Caple, Kathy.
  Starring Hillary / written and illustrated by Kathy Caple.
    p. cm.
  Summary: Hillary the cat makes herself miserable trying to lose weight for a play audition, but she finally realizes that she is just right the way she is.
  ISBN 1-57505-261-X (alk. paper)
  [1. Weight control—Fiction. 2. Actors and actresses—Fiction.
3. Self-acceptance—Fiction. 4. Cats—Fiction.] I. Title.
PZ.C17368St 1999
[E]—dc21   97-32209

Manufactured in the United States of America
1 2 3 4 5 6 – JR – 04 03 02 01 00 99

Hillary was a little on the round side.
"I wouldn't worry about it," said her mother.
"We come in all shapes and sizes. You are just right the way you are."

Hillary's older sister, Felice, was anything but round. To stay that way, Felice was always dieting. If it wasn't one diet, it was another. And she was always exercising.

"Can't you ever relax and have fun?" asked Hillary.

"I am having fun," said Felice. She put on another CD and started her aerobics.

Hillary knew how to have fun. She liked to make up plays and pretend she was onstage. "When I grow up, I'm going to be a real actress," said Hillary.

"You'll never make it, as round as you are,"
said Felice. "You need to go on a diet." Hillary
always ignored this advice.

One day Hillary saw a notice in the newspaper.

Famous Actress, Singer and Producer

Nina Clophoofer

in Town to Direct New Play

Small Part Available For Child Actress

Audition Next Saturday at the Little Theater

Hillary looked in the mirror. For the first time, she felt fat.

"Don't worry," said Felice. "You're in good hands."

That night Felice weighed all of Hillary's food.
"Is that all I get?" asked Hillary.
"I was being generous tonight," said Felice.

"Now it's time for the stairstepper."
Felice made Hillary do thirty minutes on the stairs and another thirty minutes on the exercise bike. After that it was time for the aerobics video.

The next day was even worse.

Hillary had dry toast for breakfast, watery
soup for lunch, and a bowl of lettuce for dinner.

Hillary spent every spare minute exercising.

On top of that, Felice watched her like a hawk. "No cheating," she warned one night as Hillary was about to have a little snack.

One day became another. All Hillary did anymore was exercise and go hungry.

She had
trouble
sleeping.

She was
nervous all
the time.

By the end of the week, Hillary was a wreck,
and the audition was only a day away.

"Guess what?" said Felice. "I have two tickets
for a performance by Nina Clophoofer tonight.
Let's go."

When they got to the theater, a crowd was waiting outside. A limousine pulled up.
"There's Nina Clophoofer," a lady said.
Hillary watched as Nina got out of the car.

"Nina is round," said Hillary.
"Isn't she glamorous?" said Felice.

Hillary and Felice went into the theater. The stage was dark. A spotlight came on. There was Nina.

Nina spoke and moved. She sang. She sang as if she liked herself. She looked comfortable. She was having fun.

"Isn't she cool?" said Felice.
"She's my favorite actress," said someone behind Hillary.

"All right," said Felice when the performance
was over. "It's time to get back to the
stairstepper."

"No," said Hillary. "It's time for a snack."

When Hillary got home, she went straight to the kitchen, made a peanut butter sandwich, and poured some apple juice.

"And now I'm going to study my lines," she said.

Hillary went to her room. She read the lines. She felt the lines. She moved and spoke as if she liked herself. She felt comfortable. She became the character. She had fun.

"This is more like it," Hillary said.

The next morning, Hillary put on her favorite outfit. Then she went to the kitchen. She poured some cereal, covered it with milk, and ate it.

"Delicious," said Hillary. She was ready for the audition.

Hillary went to the theater.

She stood on the stage. She liked herself.
She felt comfortable.

She became the character.

She had fun.

"I got the part!" Hillary exclaimed when she got home.

"What about your weight?" asked Felice. "I'll help you get back on the diet."

"Actually," said Hillary, "they liked me the way
I am. I figure if I eat normally from now on, I'll
be just right."

Hillary took out a whole wheat roll and made
a tuna fish sandwich.

She took a bite and smiled. It had never
tasted better.